WHEN THE Dragons CAME

To our fabulous husbands, Mike and Simon,
for all their support and encouragement,
and to Archie, Charlie, Joe and Will, our wonderful boys,
whose passion for dragons sparked this story – **NK/LM**

For Mum and Dad – **BD**

SIMON AND SCHUSTER
First published in Great Britain in 2010 by Simon and Schuster UK Ltd
1st Floor, 222 Gray's Inn Road, London WC1X 8HB
A CBS Company

Text copyright © 2010 Naomi Kefford and Lynne Moore
Illustrations copyright © 2010 Benji Davies

The right of Naomi Kefford, Lynne Moore and Benji Davies to be identified
as the authors and illustrator of this work has been asserted
by them in accordance with the Copyright, Designs and Patents Act, 1988

ISBN: 978-1-84738-303-7 (HB)
ISBN: 978-1-84738-304-4 (PB)

Printed in Singapore
1 3 5 7 9 10 8 6 4 2

WHEN THE Dragons CAME

Naomi Kefford and Lynne Moore
Illustrated by Benji Davies

SIMON AND SCHUSTER
London New York Sydney

Poppledown Town was the loveliest town.

The neat rows of houses had charming front gardens,
With hedges and lawns that were trimmed every day.
The High Street provided whatever was needed,
The riverbank was perfect for picnics in May.

Oh yes,
Poppledown Town was the LOVELIEST town.
And everyone who lived there agreed.

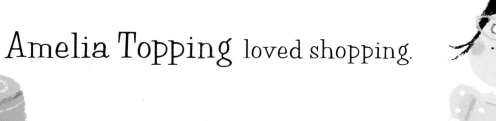

Amelia Topping loved shopping.

She skipped down the aisles
of Poppledown Market,

Selecting her salads, her cheese and cold meats.

She paused at the freezers and chose all her favourites,
Then filled up her trolley with doughnuts and treats.

Oh yes,
Amelia Topping LOVED shopping . . .

...until the **dragons** came!

SPECIAL OFFER

Frederick Creeding loved reading.

He hurried each morning to Poppledown Library,
Treasuring the hush as he browsed along rows.

He liked choosing stories then reading them quietly,
And the click of the stamp on each book that he chose.

Oh yes,

Frederick Creeding LOVED reading . . .

...until the **dragons** came!

Olivia Turning loved learning.

She sat on the carpet at
Poppledown Playgroup,

Eager for stories and songs with Miss Twee.

She carefully moulded her plasticine biscuits,
Ready to use in her Teddy Bears' Tea.

Oh yes,
Olivia Turning LOVED learning . . .

...until the **dragons** came!

Soon Olivia Turning HATED learning,
Frederick Creeding AVOIDED reading,
And Amelia Topping STOPPED shopping.

For Poppledown Town just wasn't the same –
since the dragons came.

But . . .

Jeremy Stamping LOVED camping.

He set up his tent on Poppledown Common,
A holiday village of orange and red.

He checked all the guy ropes, the pegs and the zippers,
Then sizzled his sausages and pumped up his bed.

Oh yes,
Jeremy Stamping LOVED camping...

...until the **rain** came!

It drummed on the canvas like zebras tap-dancing,
It hammered the flysheet and trickled down poles.

It seeped into sleeping bags, gathered in puddles.
The campers were soggy and hungry and cold . . .

. . . until the

dragons came!

They spread out their wings and provided a shelter,
They dried up the puddles, cooked sausages to share.
The campers saw kindness and talked with the dragons,
They realised quite quickly they HAD NOT BEEN FAIR!

They explained to the dragons just how they'd annoyed them,
With clumsy behaviour and the mess that they'd made.
The dragons said sorry, they'd meant to be friendly.
They'd try to be careful and calm if they stayed . . .

So Olivia Turning went BACK to her learning,

Frederick Creeding CONTINUED reading,

And Amelia Topping ONLY went shopping on Wednesdays . . .

...when the dragons came!